HUNGRY HYENA

Also by Mwenye Hadithi and Adrienne Kennaway

Baby Baboon
Crafty Chameleon
Greedy Zebra
Hot Hippo
Lazy Lion
Tricky Tortoise

First Edition
Published in Great Britain in 1994 by Hodder and Stoughton Children's Books

ISBN 0-316-33715-3
Library of Congress Catalog Card Number 93-86043

10 9 8 7 6 5 4 3 2 1

Printed in Belgium

HUNGRY HYENA

Mwenye Hadithi and
Adrienne Kennaway

Little, Brown and Company

Boston   New York   Toronto   London

One sunny day, at the lake where Crocodile
lived, Fish Eagle caught a shiny, fat fish.
Hungry Hyena lay in the papyrus. When he
saw the shiny, fat fish, his eyes grew small
and greedy.

Hyena called to Fish Eagle, "Is that your nest in the big Sausage tree?"

"Yes, it is," Fish Eagle replied. "Why do you ask?"

"Oh, I saw Snake climbing the tree," Hyena said. "Perhaps he is looking for eagle eggs."

So Fish Eagle flew as fast as the wind, back to her nest, leaving the shiny, fat fish behind. Hyena laughed. He picked up the fish and began to eat it.

When Fish Eagle reached her nest she saw Snake fast asleep on a rock a long way away. She gave a loud, angry screech when she saw Hyena eating her fish. And he ate every single bit of it.

Fish Eagle's screech woke slow, sleepy Pangolin, who was hanging by his scaly tail from the branch of a nearby Bead tree. Fish Eagle told Pangolin all about Hyena's sneaky trick.

"Well, I have a plan," said Pangolin sleepily. "What do hyenas like best to eat?"

"Meat," said Fish Eagle, "lots and lots of meat."

"Well, I think you can show them the biggest, sweetest piece of meat in all the world," said Pangolin. And he whispered his plan to Fish Eagle.

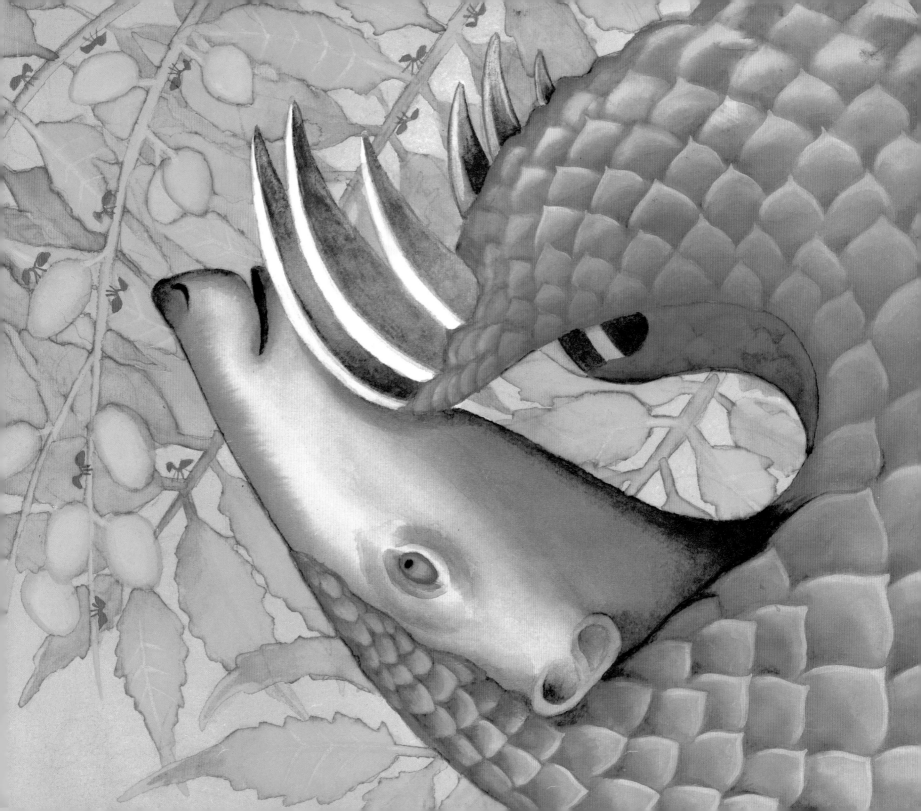

Next day Fish Eagle asked the buzzing bees for a piece of honeycomb. Then she flew to the water's edge where the animals were drinking. Hyena was pretending to be asleep.

Fish Eagle dropped the honeycomb and said loudly,
"I have found the sweetest meat in all the world."

When Hyena heard this, he ran swiftly. For in those days, he could run like the wind.

"Give it to me!" cried Hungry Hyena, and he grabbed the honeycomb and swallowed it down, every single bit of it. "Delicious! That's the sweetest meat I have ever tasted!" Hyena said, licking his lips. "I want more!"

"I know where you will find the biggest, sweetest piece of meat in all the world," said Fish Eagle. "There will be more than enough for you and your family *and* all your friends. Bring them to the lake tonight, every single one of them."

That night Fish Eagle waited with Pangolin in the Sausage tree.

They waited and they watched. And as the sun set, they saw Hyena come over the hill. Behind him was another hyena, and another, and another, until all the hyenas had come to the lake, every single one of them.

"Look at the sky!" whispered Fish Eagle.

And as the full moon rose, huge and shining, Fish Eagle called, "See! There it is! Now, climb onto each other's backs. You must climb up until you can reach the sweet meat in the sky!"

And the hyenas began to scramble onto each other's backs, climbing higher and higher and higher.

"Now, take the meat!" called Fish Eagle.
   And as the highest hyena reached out toward the moon, they all began to fall, and suddenly all the hyenas were falling out of the sky like giant raindrops.

They fell heavily. And they all fell into the lake where Crocodile lived, every single one of them. Crocodile woke up and chased them out of the water, biting their tails. And when they looked up and saw the huge, white moon shining overhead, they saw how stupid and greedy they had been, and they all limped off into the night.

From that day on Hyena could never again run like the wind, so now he slinks around on the great African plain. And Fish Eagle soars in the clouds and gives a screech when she remembers how the hyenas fell like raindrops from the sky, every single one of them. . . .